Dear Parents:

Congratulations! Your child is tak the first steps on an exciting journey. The destination? Independent reading!

STEP INTO READING® will help your child get there. The program offers five steps to reading success. Each step includes fun stories and colorful art or photographs. In addition to original fiction and books with favorite characters, there are Step into Reading Non-Fiction Readers, Phonics Readers and Boxed Sets, Sticker Readers, and Comic Readers—a complete literacy program with something to interest every child.

Learning to Read, Step by Step!

Ready to Read   Preschool–Kindergarten
• big type and easy words • rhyme and rhythm • picture clues
For children who know the alphabet and are eager to begin reading.

Reading with Help   Preschool–Grade 1
• basic vocabulary • short sentences • simple stories
For children who recognize familiar words and sound out new words with help.

Reading on Your Own   Grades 1–3
• engaging characters • easy-to-follow plots • popular topics
For children who are ready to read on their own.

Reading Paragraphs   Grades 2–3
• challenging vocabulary • short paragraphs • exciting stories
For newly independent readers who read simple sentences with confidence.

Ready for Chapters   Grades 2–4
• chapters • longer paragraphs • full-color art
For children who want to take the plunge into chapter books but still like colorful pictures.

STEP INTO READING® is designed to give every child a successful reading experience. The grade levels are only guides; children will progress through the steps at their own speed, developing confidence in their reading.

Remember, a lifetime love of reading starts with a single step!

Manufactured under license granted to AMEET Sp. z o.o.
by the LEGO Group.

AMEET Sp. z o.o.
Nowe Sady 6, 94–102 Łódź—Poland
ameet@ameet.eu
www.ameet.eu

www.LEGO.com

Published in the United States by Random House Children's Books, a division of Penguin Random House
LLC, 1745 Broadway, New York, NY 10019, and in Canada by Penguin Random House Canada Limited,
Toronto.

Visit us on the Web!
StepIntoReading.com
rhcbooks.com

Educators and librarians, for a variety of teaching tools, visit us at RHTeachersLibrarians.com

ISBN 978-0-593-57120-0 (trade)
ISBN 978-0-593-57220-7 (lib. bdg.)
ISBN 978-0-593-57121-7 (ebook)

MANUFACTURED IN CHINA

10 9 8 7 6 5 4 3 2 1

Random House Children's Books supports the First Amendment and celebrates the right to read.

Meet the Astronaut

by Steve Foxe

based on the story by Erica S. Perl

illustrated by AMEET Studio

Random House New York

Madison Yea and Billy McCloud worked for their school newspaper.

Madison Yea
reporter

Billy McCloud
photographer

One reader asked them to write about astronauts, so Madison and Billy contacted someone very special to help with their story.

Madison and Billy soon went
to the Space Center.
They couldn't believe
they were about to meet
a famous astronaut!
A man in uniform greeted them.
Billy snapped a quick picture.
"You must be the reporters,"
the man said. "My name is
Captain Momentous,
and I am an astronaut!"

"Our readers would love to learn
about your job," Madison said.

"Sure," said Captain Momentous.

"Let's take a tour."

He led them into a gym
at the Space Center.

"This is Lieutenant Rivera,"
he said, pointing to a
woman running on a treadmill.
"I help our astronauts
stay in shape!" she huffed.

Next, Captain Momentous
took Billy and Madison
to the research center.
"Dr. Ravenhurst and Dr. Wexler
are our top scientists.
And Fred is our rocket engineer.
He helps design our spacecraft."

"Every button has a purpose,"
explained Fred,
"whether it's heating
up dinner or opening
a hatch."

"Follow me," said

Captain Momentous.

"I have a surprise for you kids."

Soon they were standing

inside a real rocket!

Captain Momentous beamed.

"This is where we train

and work together," he said.

"This tour is out of

this world!" said Madison.

"Look at me—I'm floating in space!"
said Billy, jumping up and down.
While waving his arms, he
accidentally bumped into
the control panel.
The rocket began to shake!

A voice came over the intercom:
"Captain, do you read me?
Joanne at Mission Control here.
You're about to launch
to Planet Zing!"

"Planet Zing!" exclaimed Madison.
"Buckle up, because Billy has
jump-started the rocket!"
said the captain.
"I'm sorry!" cried Billy.

"Accidents happen," replied
Captain Momentous.
"We'll work as a team
to make this unexpected
mission a success.
It's the astronaut way!"

Liftoff! The spaceship zipped through the starry sky.

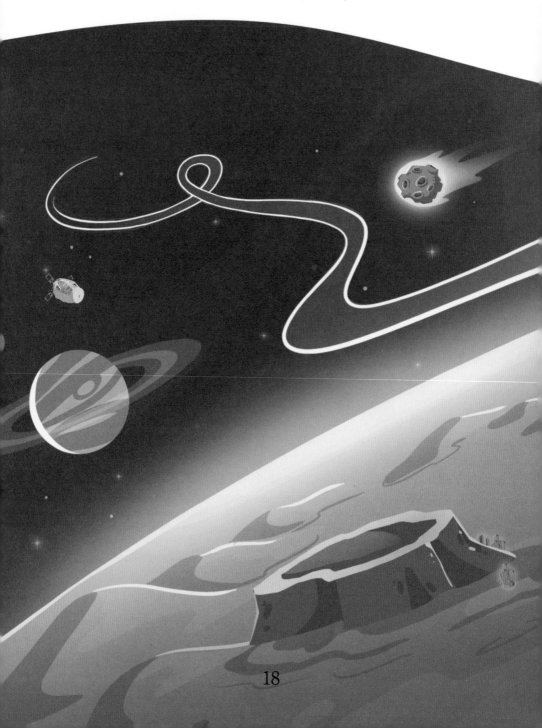

When it was time to land,
the rocket rattled before
coming to a sudden stop
on an orange planet.

Madison looked out the window.
"Captain? What's that
shimmery pink stuff?" she asked.
"Our landing must have
disturbed Zing's surface.
I'm going to have a look,"
the captain replied.

"Dr. Wexler would love to have
a new mineral sample!"
He put on his space suit.
"Mission control," he called.
"Preparing to exit and explore."

Billy and Madison watched
the captain as he crossed
the planet's surface.
Suddenly, Madison noticed him
waving his arms wildly.
"A new dance?" asked Billy.

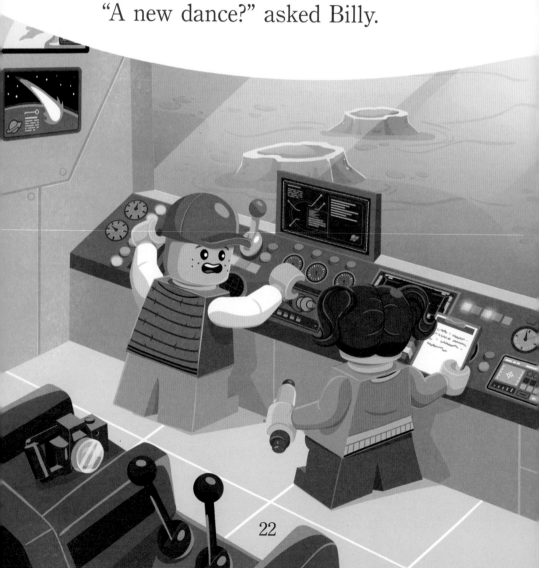

"No, I think he needs help,"
Madison replied.

"He's stuck in that crater!"

"We can't help," Billy said.

"We're not astronauts!"

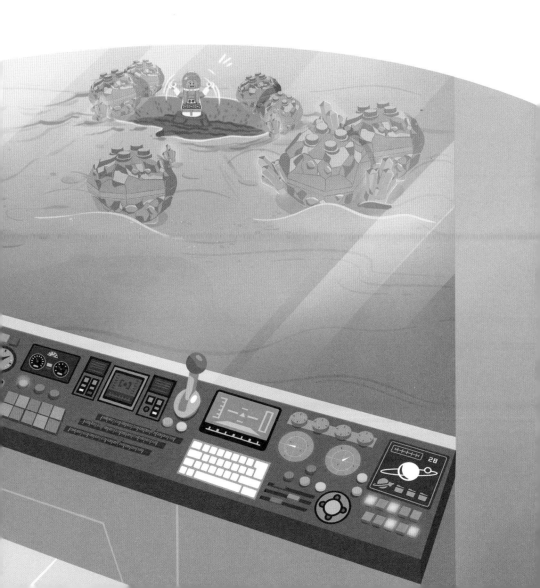

"What about the rover?"
Madison asked. "We can
use the remote controls."
"I knew my gaming skills
would be handy one day!"
replied Billy.

Madison and Billy slowly guided
the vehicle over to the captain.
They carefully lifted him
from the crater to the ship.

Once the captain was back
aboard the spacecraft,
Madison and Billy high-fived.

"I'm so glad you both were here,"
the captain said, holding up
bottles of sparkling minerals.
"You saved me, and the samples, too."
"Nice bling, Planet Zing!"
Billy remarked.

Captain Momentous checked
all the controls, then launched
the rocket back to Earth.
Everyone at the Space Center
cheered when the spacecraft
landed safely.

Captain Momentous smiled.
"When you least expect it,
extraordinary things happen!"

"You mean like finding the space minerals?" Billy asked.

"Yes," said the captain.

"And also how you helped save me, like real astronauts." Billy and Madison couldn't wait to get back to the newspaper office and write their story about the exciting life of an astronaut.

"Working together might be
the astronaut way,
but it's also the reporter way,"
Madison said thoughtfully.
"That's true," Billy said, nodding.
"And researching this story
was truly . . . momentous!"